Lunch Munch

A Ready, Set, Go! Reader

by **Liza Charlesworth**
illustrated by Mark Chambers

ISBN 978-0-545-79571-5

12 11 10 9 8 7 6 5 4 3 2 1   14 15 16 17 18 19

Printed in the U.S.A.   40
First printing, September 2014

Designed by Maria Mercado

SCHOLASTIC INC.

It is time for lunch.

I have a sandwich.
Munch, munch!

I have a carrot.
Crunch, crunch!

I have a burger.
Munch, munch!

I have a taco.
Crunch, crunch!

I have a pizza.
Munch, munch!

I have a pretzel.
Crunch, crunch!

I have a dumpling.
Munch, munch!

I have an apple.
Crunch, crunch!

I have a banana.
Munch, munch!

I have a cookie
to share with a friend.

Crunch, crunch!

Munch, munch!
Crunch, crunch!

We munch and crunch our lunch!

Comprehension Boosters

1. What different foods did the children eat?

2. Why is the lunchroom so noisy?

3. What is *your* favorite thing to eat for lunch?